Andrew Henry's Meadow

To most everyone, Andrew Henry Thatcher's enthusiasm for building things was a nuisance. Even the helicopter in the kitchen and the merry-go-round hitched to the sewing machine seemed to get in the way. So, one day, Andrew Henry quietly packed and moved to a meadow.

Before long Alice Burdock, who liked birds, turned up. Her father didn't care for birds. Then George Turner came along with his boats and paddle wheel. And soon, six other children, each with a special interest that nobody seemed to appreciate.

How Andrew Henry aroused the whole town, and accidentally found a happy solution to his problem, is a captivating story. Almost more absorbing are the detailed drawings of his ingenious and quite buildable inventions.

Doris Burn's writing skill matches her talent as an artist. Combining a delicious understanding of childish longings and a gift for comical understatement, she creates a picture book sure to become a dog-eared favorite of both parents and children.

Andrew Henry's Meadow

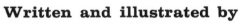

Written and illustrated by
Doris Burn

Coward—McCann Inc.
New York

This book is lovingly dedicated to
Robin, Mark, Cameron and Lisa.

Library of Congress Catalog Card Number: 65-20384
MANUFACTURED IN THE UNITED STATES OF AMERICA
Weekly Reader Children's Book Club Edition. Primary Division.

Until that spring Andrew Henry Thatcher
lived with his family in the town of Stubbsville.

He had a father and mother and two older sisters
named Marian and Martha. The girls were always
with each other. He also had two younger brothers
named Robert and Ronald.
They were always with each other too.
Andrew Henry was in the middle.
He was always with himself,
yet he didn't mind.
He had plenty of things to do.

Mrs. Thatcher was usually busy in the kitchen,
but Mr. Thatcher was tired when he came home from work.
He liked to read the paper and have things quiet.
Marian and Martha liked to sew
or try new ways to wear their hair.
Robert and Ronald liked to play
with toy cars and coloring books.

But Andrew Henry liked to build things.

Mrs. Thatcher was unhappy when Andrew Henry
built a helicopter in the kitchen.
The helicopter had many fine features.

Nevertheless, she said to him firmly,
"Andrew Henry, I have work to do.
You must take that thing out of the kitchen."

Then Andrew Henry built an eagle's cage in the living room,
and Mr. Thatcher was annoyed. It was a fine eagle's cage.
An eagle would have liked it, but Mr. Thatcher didn't.

He told Andrew Henry to go outside
and to take the eagle's cage with him.

When Marian and Martha saw the merry-go-round
Andrew Henry had hitched up to the sewing machine,
they were upset. It went around nicely too.
But they told him to unhitch it
and to do it "right now."

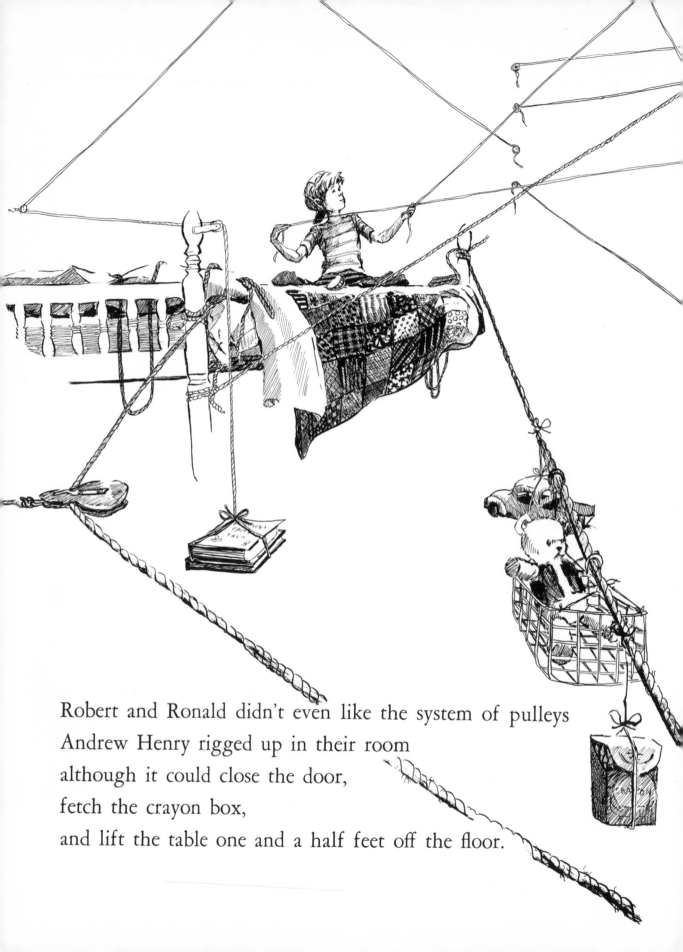

Robert and Ronald didn't even like the system of pulleys
Andrew Henry rigged up in their room
although it could close the door,
fetch the crayon box,
and lift the table one and a half feet off the floor.

They cried,
"You're always spoiling our fun, Andrew Henry.
Leave us alone."

Andrew Henry thought about it more and more.
One fine spring morning he made up his mind.
Quietly he gathered together his tools.
He packed his hammer and his saw,
his pocket knife and pliers,
a big sack of nails,
some bolts, nuts, and wire,
and even a few lengths
of stovepipe.

"I'll build a house for myself," he said to himself.
He went out the back door and down the path.
He knew where he was going.

No one saw Andrew Henry leave
except the Thatcher's dog, Sam.
As usual Sam started to follow Andrew Henry,
but this time Andrew Henry told him firmly
that he must stay home.

Sam was a good dog.
So he sat down by the gate in the shade of the lilac bush
and watched until Andrew Henry was out of sight.

Andrew Henry walked kitty-corner through Burdock's pasture

and climbed up over Blackbriar Hill.

Then he went out across Worzibsky's Swamp

and in through the deep woods.

Finally he came to a meadow.

A stream wandered through the meadow,
sparkling in the sunlight.

On one side was a tall fir tree, straight and strong.

Andrew Henry walked right over to the fir tree.
He dropped his tools beside it
and looked the ground over.
"Here is where I'll build my house," he said to himself.

He set to work, and before long the house was finished.
The walls were made of clay and rocks and poles.
The roof was made of fir boughs,
and outside one window
there was a fine landing field for dragonflies.

But Andrew Henry wasn't alone long.
Soon Alice Burdock stepped out from the deep woods.
She had her bird things with her.
Mr. Burdock, who was a farmer, didn't care for birds.
They ate his cherries, scratched up his corn
and nested in his barn.

He put scarecrows in the cornfield and tied tin cans
in the cherry trees to scare away the birds.
He even kept four cats in the barn
to discourage the swallows from nesting there.
But Alice liked birds.
She had brought along what she could.
"Andrew Henry, will you build me a house too?" she asked.
"Sure thing," Andrew Henry said.

It was a nice house,
especially for a person who liked birds.
A ladder climbed straight up the trunk
of the old tree to the house.

There were plenty of birdbaths and feeding stations.
There were birdhouses and a balcony for watching birds
and even a handy rest for Alice's binoculars
when she wasn't using them.

Next, out of the deep woods came George Turner.
He had most of his boats, all of his fishing poles
and his biggest paddle wheel.
Mrs. Turner didn't like him
to use these things in the bathtub.
George wanted Andrew Henry
to build him a house too.
"Sure thing," Andrew Henry said.

First they built a bridge over the creek.
Then they built the house on the bridge
so that George could be near the water.

The house had docks for the boats and built-in fishing poles.
The paddle wheel worked a fan to keep George cool.
It was surprising how much power that paddle wheel had.

Then Joe Polasky arrived. They built him a dugout house.
The door was on the roof and the chimney
stuck out of the ground. Joe wanted an underground house
so that his pets would be comfortable.
He had gray mice and white mice,
a pet mole and a pair of brown rabbits.
The house had rooms and passageways for his pets.
The mole's passageways were wonderfully misleading.

Jane O'Malley and Margot LaPorte showed up next.
Andrew Henry built Jane a house that looked
like a castle with turrets. They dug a ditch around it
which filled up with water from the creek.
The ditch made a useful moat, especially
when the drawbridge was up.

Jane had her dress-up clothes with her.
She hoped her mother wouldn't miss them too much.
She explained that they made her feel
like Lady Jane instead of just plain Jane.

Margot's house was tall in the middle like a teepee,
but it had a long, low entrance like an igloo.
She needed privacy for her music.

Visitors had to crawl in on their stomachs.
They also had to give three "toots"
on the horn she had hung beside the door.
Sometimes Margot didn't answer
because she couldn't always hear the horn
when she was practicing.

Down the hill, across the swamp and into the woods
came three more children.

Sarah Lerner had a cookie sheet full of mud cakes
her mother had made her take out of the oven.

Don Peterson had a dresser drawer full of dandelion seeds
he had been saving to use for parachutes.

Stanley Hayes had the two racing toads
his father wouldn't let him keep in the basement.

Soon nine houses stood in the meadow.

It looked like a small village.

But in Stubbsville
the Thatchers were looking for Andrew Henry,
and the Burdocks were looking for Alice.
Soon the Turners, the Polaskys,
the O'Malleys and LaPortes,
the Lerners, the Petersons, and Hayes
all began looking for the missing children.

For four days and four nights everyone searched frantically.
They hunted in the fields and the barns,
the buildings and the vacant lots.
But the children could not be found.

The only one who wasn't searching
was the Thatcher's dog Sam.
He sat quietly under the lilac bush by the gate.
Sam was a good dog but he was very lonesome.
As he gazed sorrowfully out
toward the far corner of Burdock's pasture,
the lonesomeness in Sam grew and grew and grew.
Finally it grew too big for even a good dog.

On the morning of the fifth day
Sam raised his head and out poured a long, aching howl.

He sprang to his feet and raced for the near corner
of Burdock's pasture. The townspeople all heard the howl
and saw Sam racing off with his nose to the ground.
"The dog has found their trail!"
"Follow Sam!"
"Hooray for Sam!"
Sam ran kitty-corner
through Burdock's pasture.
The fathers and the mothers,
the sisters and the brothers,
even the cats and the dogs
of the missing children,
all ran kitty-corner after him.

They climbed up over Blackbriar Hill
and went across Worzibsky's Swamp —

and in through the deep woods

until they came to a meadow.
It was Andrew Henry's meadow.

There were the children.

What excitement!
The nine children, their parents
and all their sisters and brothers met with shouts of joy.
They laughed and hugged each other.
The fathers and mothers were too happy to scold
or to ask any questions.
Their children were safe.

Andrew Henry and his friends were happy too.
They had been away from home for four long days
and four very long nights.
The village in the meadow had been wonderful.
They would not forget it.
But they missed their mothers and fathers,
their sisters and brothers
and their cats and dogs.
They were ready to go home.

The Thatchers gave Andrew Henry
the corner of the basement behind the furnace
just to build things in.
He built a roller coaster for Robert and Ronald's toy cars.
By using a bucket and parts of an electric fan,
he made a hair dryer for Marian and Martha.
The pipe filler he made for his father
worked the same way a bird feeder does.
And he was especially proud of the automatic table setter
he made for his mother, although it did take up a lot of room.
Andrew Henry was pleased to have such a fine place to work.

And his family was always curious to see
what Andrew Henry would build next.

The Author

Since she was nine years old and first set foot on a small island in Puget Sound, DORIS BURN wanted to live on an island.

She lived in Portland, Oregon, where she was born, and she attended the Universities of Oregon, Hawaii and Washington, where she received her degree, before she found her island home where she lives today.

Andrew Henry's Meadow was created on Waldron in Washington. The island has no electricity, telephones, running water, or stores of any kind. Everything has to be brought in on the mail boat from the mainland, including the paper, pens, brushes and inks for her work.

Mrs. Burn's studio is a small cabin where she spends the day at work after chopping enough wood to keep the fire going through the day, hauling two buckets of water from the pump for washing brushes and pens and brewing "a perpetual pot of tea." She looks out on the channel and the beautiful Canadian islands.

Her four children attend the island's one-room schoolhouse where she previously taught for a year.